Cont

Chapter 1
Wedding Plans

It was Saturday morning and Holly was baking a chocolate cake. Her sister Mia danced into the kitchen in her PJs.

"Guess what happened last night?" she said. "James asked me to marry him!"

Holly put the cake in the oven. "And what did you say?" she asked.

Mia grinned. "I said 'YES,' of course. We're getting married in the summer!"

"Have you told Mum and Dad?" asked Holly.

Mia shook her head. "Not yet. James is coming round soon. We'll tell them together."

"You'd better get dressed then," Holly said.

Mia laughed and danced upstairs. Holly started to mix some chocolate icing. 'I wonder what Mum and Dad will say,' she thought.

Dad was worried at first. "You're only 19," he said to Mia and James. "That's very young to get married."

"But they're sensible," said Mum. "And they've both got good jobs. I think it's lovely!"

Mum gave Mia a hug. And then she hugged James as well. "Let's have some of Holly's chocolate cake!" she said.

Holly cut everyone a big slice of cake. While they ate it, they talked about the wedding.

"We want to invite all our friends," said Mia. "And everyone in our families too."

"Hang on," said Dad. "Weddings cost a lot of money. How many people is that?"

"Let's make a list," said James. He took out his pen and he and Mia wrote down all their friends' names.

"And there's our mums and dads," said Mia. "And Holly."

"Don't forget Auntie Alice," Mum said. "And all your cousins."

James wrote them all down. "And we *must* invite my football team," he said.

"And the girls from work," said Mia.

They kept thinking of more and more people. By the time they'd eaten their cake, there were a hundred names on the list.

When Dad counted the names, he went pale. "We can't afford it," he said.

"James and I have been saving," said Mia. "We can pay for some of the food."

"It's not just the food," Dad said. "There's the dress too. And the hotel and the cars and – "

Mum patted Dad's hand. "Don't worry," she said. "I'll make the dress. And we don't need to book a hotel. We'll have a big tent in the garden."

Holly grinned. "Uncle David will take the photos," she said. "And maybe Sally will do the flowers." Sally was the owner of the flower shop where Mia worked.

James nodded. "My boss will lend us some cars," he said. (James worked in a garage.) "And I'll ask my mum and my Auntie Kate to do the meal. They love cooking – except for cakes."

"There's got to be a *cake*!" Holly said. "It won't be a proper wedding without a wedding cake."

Mia sighed. "We can't have everything," she said. "We've got to be sensible. We'll manage without a cake."

"I could *make* a cake," said Holly.

Everyone laughed and Mum shook her head. "You're a good cook, Holly," she said, "but wedding cakes are hard to make. And we'd need a *huge* one for all those people. Mia's right. They'll have to manage without one."

'No they won't!' Holly thought. Everyone loved her cakes. Her sponges were light. Her fruit cakes were super-fruity. And her brownies were bursting with chocolate. She knew she could make a great wedding cake for Mia and James.

But she didn't say anything. 'It can be a surprise,' she thought.

She fetched the rest of the chocolate cake. "Anyone want any more?" she said.

And everyone said, "YES!"

That night, Holly couldn't sleep. She tossed and turned, thinking about the wedding cake. She knew how to make swiss rolls and jam tarts, flapjacks and lemon drizzle cakes. And everyone said her cupcakes were the best in the world. But a wedding cake had to be *special*.

How would she make it?

After three hours of tossing and turning, Holly gave up trying to sleep. She got up and went downstairs to make a hot drink.

Mia had left a wedding magazine on the kitchen table. Holly sat down and opened it. The first thing she saw was a picture of a big, white wedding cake with five layers. It was covered with fancy icing and hundreds of sugar flowers.

'HELP!' she thought. 'I don't know how to make those!'

Then she turned the page. There was a different kind of wedding cake. This one was a tall stand with ten layers, like a tower. But these layers were full of pretty little pink and white *cupcakes*!

'That's better!' Holly thought. 'I can make those!'

But there were going to be a hundred people at the wedding. That meant a lot of cupcakes. She might need some help with the baking. She took out her phone and sent a text to Poppy and Tom, her best friends.

Got something 2 show u. Cum 2 my house be4 school.

Then she went back to bed and fell fast asleep.

Chapter 2

HOW Many Cakes???

Next morning Holly was still eating her toast when the bell rang. Mum went to open the door.

"Poppy and Tom are here!" she shouted.

Holly swallowed the rest of the toast and raced into the hall. Poppy and Tom were standing at the front door.

"What's up?" Poppy said. "What have you got to show us?"

"Ssh!" said Holly. "It's a secret. Wait a minute."

She fetched Mia's magazine and showed them the cupcake tower. "I want to make one of these," she whispered. "For Mia's wedding."

"Mia's getting **married**?" Poppy screeched. "What's she going to **wear**?"

"Mum's making her dress," Holly said. "And there's a hundred people coming to the wedding. Will you help me make a cupcake tower – as a surprise?"

"Of course!" said Poppy. "But we'll need a LOT of cupcakes."

"And a stand," said Tom. He was looking hard at the picture. "Do you think they cost a lot of money?"

"Let's look on the internet," said Holly. "We can do it at lunch time."

At lunch time, Holly, Poppy and Tom went to the school library to use a computer. There were lots of stands for sale on the internet. But they all cost loads of money.

"And they're too small anyway," Poppy said. "They won't hold enough cakes."

"How many will we need?" said Tom. "We'd better work it out."

"Well," said Holly, "there's a hundred people coming to the wedding ..."

Poppy tried to work it out on her fingers. "How many cupcakes does one person eat?"

"Three?" said Holly.

Poppy shook her head. "More than that. I can eat four."

"I can eat ten!" said Tom.

Holly gasped. "**Ten**???"

"At least," said Tom. "People always eat lots of cupcakes. Especially at weddings."

"If we make ten cakes for everyone ..." Poppy counted on her fingers. "We need ... we need ..."

"We need a *huge* stand to put them on," said Tom. "Where are we going to get one that big?"

"I can make one," said a voice from the next computer.

It was Bella, the school maths whizz. As the others watched, she drew a stand on her computer screen. It was like a very tall tower.

"I'll use old metal trays to make it," she said. "You'll need at least 25 layers to hold all those cupcakes."

"So how many cupcakes will we need?" said Holly.

Bella looked at them all.

"You'll need a **thousand**!" she said.

Chapter 3

How Much MONEY???

"A thousand cupcakes!" Poppy screeched. "How can we make that many?"

"You'll have to get everyone in the class to help," said Bella.

"They'll never do that," said Tom.

But Holly had an idea. "Maybe they will," she said. "Let me talk to them all after lunch."

So they ate their lunch and then raced back to the classroom. Holly waited until the whole class was there, and jumped up on the table at the front.

"This is about **cake**!" she shouted.

That made everyone stop talking.

"What cake?" asked Joe. (Joe was always eating.)

"I'm making my sister's wedding cake," Holly said. "And I want you to help me."

"Why should we?" said Joe.

Holly looked round the class. There were 25 people in the room.

"I want you all to bake 48 cupcakes," she said. "On the day before the wedding. I'll buy all the stuff to make them. You'll give 40 to me for the wedding and keep the other 8 for yourselves. So you get **8 free cupcakes**! What do you say?"

"What about the icing?" asked Joe.

"I'll do that," Holly said.

"And I'll decorate the cakes," said Poppy. "I'll make them *really* pretty."

There was a lot of muttering, all over the room. Then Bella jumped onto the table next to Holly. She had printed out her picture of the cupcake stand and she held it up for everyone to see.

"I'm going to make a tower like this for the cakes," she shouted. "And it's going to be *4 metres tall!*"

Everyone gasped. "That's awesome," said Joe. "It'll be the tallest wedding cake in the world."

All of a sudden, everyone was excited about the wedding cake. They all wanted to help. Holly grinned and held up her hands.

"That's fantastic!" she said. "But you mustn't tell anyone else. It's a **secret**. OK?"

"OK!" everyone shouted back.

Holly grinned and jumped off the table – just in time. Two seconds later, Mrs Bennett walked in.

So now there were 25 cooks and Holly thought everything was sorted. But Bella was still doing sums. At the end of the day, she came to find Holly and her friends.

"You need a lot of stuff for 1,000 cupcakes," she said. "Look." And she held out a list. It said:

8 1/2 kilos margarine
8 1/2 kilos caster sugar
21 kilos icing sugar
8 1/2 kilos flour
10 1/2 kilos butter
168 eggs

"Wow!" gasped Poppy. "How much will all that cost?"

"I checked it out on the internet," Bella said. She looked down at her sums. "It comes to £121.80."

"A hundred and twenty-one pounds!!!" Tom said.

Bella nodded. "And 80 pence."

"Where are we going to get that kind of money?" said Holly.

"Will your mum and dad give you some?" asked Tom.

"I don't want to ask them," Holly said. "I want it to be a *surprise*. We'll have to raise the money somehow."

"How about a car boot sale?" said Poppy. "There's a big one on Saturday and my mum loves them. She'll take us. Bring all your old stuff to sell."

Holly went through all her cupboards and found enough old toys to fill two bags. On Saturday, she and Tom went round to Poppy's house. Bella was there as well, with three old calculators and a box of Lego.

Poppy came out with ten big carrier bags. "I've packed up all my old clothes," she said.

'Fantastic!' thought Holly. 'We can sell those for a lot of money.' Poppy always had beautiful designer clothes.

Poppy's mum came out of the house. "Wow!" she said when she saw all the bags. "It's a good thing I've got a big car."

The bags filled the boot and most of the back seat. Poppy sat in front with her mum and Holly squeezed into the back. The others waved them off.

"Make lots of money!" Bella shouted.

"Make a *million pounds*!" yelled Tom.

"We don't need a million pounds," Holly yelled back. "Just one hundred and twenty-one."

"And 80 pence," shouted Bella.

Chapter 4

Celebrities
– of the Car Boot Sale

They drove about twenty miles to the car boot sale. There were hundreds of people there already, selling things that looked brand new – games consoles and CDs and smartphones. Holly's heart sank. Who was going to buy her old toys with stuff like that around?

Poppy's mum unfolded a camping table and Holly and Poppy laid out the toys and the calculators. But they didn't sell anything. People didn't even bother to stop and look. "That's all rubbish," Holly heard one of them say.

'What are we going to do?' Holly thought. 'We won't make any money at all.'

But Poppy's mum was unpacking the clothes. "We should hang them up," she said. "Then people can see how good they are."

She found a piece of string and tied one end to her car. The man next to them let her tie the other end to his van and they pegged Poppy's clothes all along the string. They flapped in the wind and people started looking.

"I'll give you a pound for that dress," one woman said.

Holly was going to say yes, but Poppy trod on her foot to stop her.

"It's a designer label," she said to the woman. "It costs loads more than that."

The woman frowned. "I'll give you two pounds," she said.

"Ten," said Poppy.

"Five pounds," said the woman.

"Five pounds *and 80 pence*," said Poppy. "We're raising money to make Holly's sister a wedding cake."

The woman stopped frowning and smiled at Holly. "How sweet!" she said. "I'll give you six pounds for the dress. It's really nice of you to sell your lovely clothes to help your sister."

"They're not – " Holly started to say.

Poppy trod on her foot again. "Sssh!" she said. "I've got an idea."

"What?" said Holly.

Poppy shook her head. "Never mind. Just stand in front of the clothes – and keep your mouth shut."

Holly heard her asking her mum for a pen and a piece of paper. But she didn't see what she did with them – because all of a sudden there was a flood of people at their car. Lots of women stopped to look at Poppy's clothes. And they *all smiled at Holly.*

Holly didn't have to sell anything herself, because Poppy was right behind her. Every time one of the women picked out a dress or a top, Poppy said, "Ten pounds" or "Five pounds" – and the women paid what she asked! Without arguing!

In half an hour, they'd sold all the clothes. Poppy counted the money. "We've made a hundred and fifty pounds!" she said. "We'll be able to buy decorations for the cakes as well."

"I don't understand," Holly said. "Why did people pay so much?"

"Because I'm clever," said Poppy. "Look!"

Holly turned round and saw the notice Poppy had stuck up on the car. It said:

PLEASE BUY THESE CLOTHES!
I NEED MONEY FOR MY SISTER'S WEDDING CAKE!

"That's really embarrassing!" Holly said. "How *could* you?"

"It worked, didn't it?" Poppy grinned. "And it made people pay more for the clothes. Now we – "

She broke off in the middle of what she was saying and grabbed Holly's arm.

"Oh no!" she said. "Look who's here!"

Holly turned round – and saw Mia and James, walking towards them.

"Help!" she said. "They mustn't see me!" She snatched the notice off the car and dived into the back seat. Poppy slammed the door shut behind her.

They were just in time. A couple of seconds later, Mia and James came across to the car.

"Hello, Poppy," Mia said. "Fancy seeing you here!"

"We – er – we love car boot sales," Poppy said. "Don't we, Mum?"

Poppy's mum smiled at Mia and James. "I hear you're getting married. That's very brave when you're so young."

"We're not *that* young," James said.

"We'll be 20 soon," said Mia.

Holly peeped at them over the top of the back seat. They were walking off – and they were both frowning.

When they'd gone, Poppy opened the door to let Holly out. "That was a close shave!" she said. "If they'd seen my notice, it would have ruined the surprise."

"But they didn't see it," Holly said. "And we've got the money we need. We can go shopping!"

Chapter 5

Secret Shopping

Three days before the wedding, Holly went shopping with Poppy and Tom. They loaded their trolley with sugar and flour, eggs and butter and margarine. It was very heavy.

"It weighs more than me!" Poppy said.

"We've got quite a lot of money left," Tom said. "We can buy really nice decorations."

"Woo-hoo!" said Poppy. "Pretty things!"

They chose sugar flowers and butterflies and little silver balls. They were just picking out colours for the icing when Tom muttered, "*Look out!*"

He shot off, taking the trolley with him.

"Hey!" shouted Holly.

She and Poppy raced after him. They found him up at the back of the shop, by the cat food.

"What are you doing?" said Poppy.

"Hiding," whispered Tom. "Mia and James have just come into the shop. They mustn't see what's in this trolley."

"OK," said Poppy. "I'll go and head them off. Pay for the stuff and get out of here as fast as you can!"

Poppy ran off down the shop. Holly peered round the corner and saw her crash into the trolley James was pushing.

"Careful!" James said.

"Where are you going, Poppy?" asked Mia.

"I'm looking for the – um – the car polish," said Poppy. "Do you know where it is?"

"Of course," said James. He knew everything about cars. "I'll show you."

While James and Mia were taking Poppy to the car polish, Tom and Holly ran to the checkout. They paid for all their shopping and loaded it into bags. But it was much too heavy to carry.

"Push the trolley into the car park!" said Tom. "I'll phone my brother and ask him to pick us up."

Tom's brother was there in ten minutes and they loaded the shopping into his car. Then he and Tom took it home and Holly went back into the shop to look for Poppy.

Poppy was standing by the car polish with James and Mia. They were talking to an old man with a grumpy face.

"James and Mia are getting *married*," Poppy was saying. "Isn't that wonderful?"

"Hmmph!" said the grumpy man. "They don't look old enough."

"We're 19," Mia said.

"Much too young!" said the grumpy man. "You'll never cope on your own."

Mia went pale and James put his arm round her. "We'll be fine!" he said. But he didn't sound very happy.

Holly waved at Poppy, to show her the danger was over. Poppy gave James and Mia a big smile. "I don't think my dad uses this kind of car polish," she said. "I'll have to look somewhere else."

She danced away down the shop and she and Holly met in the car park.

"Now to get everyone cooking!" Holly said.

Chapter 6

The Great Bake

Holly, Poppy and Tom took the shopping into school next morning and Holly shared it out among the class.

"You need to bake the cakes on Friday afternoon," she said. "That way they'll be fresh for the wedding on Saturday."

"I don't know how to make cakes," said Joe. "You'll have to show me."

"And me!" said lots of other people.

Holly frowned. "How can I show you all at once?" She didn't know what to do.

But Bella did. "You'll have to make a video," she said. "And post it on YouTube."

So that's what Holly did. On Thursday, her Mum and Dad went bowling and Mia went out with James. As soon as they'd all gone, Bella took her webcam round to Holly's house.

"I'll shoot the video," she said. "You just make the cakes – and explain what you're doing while you're doing it."

It was difficult to talk and cook at the same time. It took Holly much longer than usual to make the cupcakes. She was only just taking them out of the oven when the front door opened.

"It's Mia!" hissed Bella. "Hide the cakes!"

Holly pushed them back into the oven and slammed the door shut. A second later, Mia walked into the kitchen.

She sniffed. "What's that smell?"

"It's – um – my new perfume," said Bella.

"Smells like cake," Mia said.

Bella nodded. "It's called *Yummy*."

Holly laughed – but Mia didn't. She looked upset.

"What's the matter?" Holly asked.

"Nothing," Mia said, a bit too fast. "I think I'll go to bed." She ran upstairs and slammed her bedroom door.

"Do you think she's OK?" whispered Bella.

Holly didn't answer – because she smelt the cakes burning. When she opened the oven door, she saw twelve black lumps.

"You'd better not video those!" she said. And she threw them in the bin.

Bella posted the video on YouTube – and it worked! Everyone watched it, and on Friday afternoon they were all ready to start baking.

When the cakes were cooked, Holly and Poppy went round to all the houses to decorate them. Holly piped pink and white icing on top of them. Poppy added flowers and butterflies and silver balls.

They looked *beautiful*.

When they reached Bella's house, she opened the door and beamed at them.

"My cakes are ready," she said. "But that's not all. Come and see the stand!"

It was out in the garage – and it was awesome. It was so tall they had to stand on a chair to see the top. And it was all painted silver.

"It comes to bits," Bella said. "So my mum and I can bring it round in the car. Where do you want it?"

"Mum and Dad are putting up a tent in the back garden," Holly said. "That's where it has to go."

"We'll come round as soon as it's dark," Bella said.

"And I'll phone everyone," said Poppy. "And tell them to bring their cakes."

"Good!" said Holly. "I'll go and help Mum and Dad with the tent."

Holly went straight home – but she didn't help with the tent. Because when she let herself

into the house, Mia was sitting on the stairs. She was wearing her wedding dress, and she looked fantastic.

Except for one thing.

She was in floods of tears.

Chapter 7

I Can't Do It!

"What's the matter?" Holly ran across and sat down beside Mia. "Don't cry. You're getting married tomorrow!"

"No, I'm not!" Mia wailed. "I can't do it!"

"Why not?" said Holly. "Have you quarrelled with James?"

Mia shook her head.

Holly didn't understand. "So don't you love him any more?"

"Of course I love him!" Mia sobbed. "He's the best person in the whole world!"

"What's the problem then?" asked Holly.

Mia sniffed and wiped her eyes. "Getting married is a *huge* thing," she said. "I think everyone's right. We're too young. We'll never manage on our own."

"Of course you will!" Holly said. "You're both really sensible."

"I don't *feel* sensible," Mia wailed. She stood up. "I'm going to phone James and call off the wedding."

"No!" Holly screeched. "You can't do that!" Inside she was thinking, 'what will I do with a thousand cupcakes if there's no wedding???'

Holly jumped up and grabbed Mia's arm. "Look – you're just a bit nervous, that's all. Give yourself time to think. Don't do anything for an hour. OK?"

Mia hesitated. "Well, maybe – "

Holly gave her a big hug. "That's sensible!" she said. "Wait till I come back." And she ran off to get her bike.

Holly biked through the dark, desperate to reach James before Mia phoned him.

When she got to his house, she leaned her bike against the garden wall and walked up the path. She was just going to knock on the front door when she heard a noise beside her.

It was James. He was sitting under a tree with his head in his hands. Even in the dark, she could see he wasn't happy.

"What's the matter?" she said.

James lifted his head. "Oh Holly, I'm so unhappy!"

'Oh no!' Holly thought. "But you're getting married tomorrow!" she said.

James shook his head. "We can't do it. It's not right."

Mia's heart sank. "You don't like Mia any more?" she asked.

"Of course I do!" James said crossly. "She's the most beautiful, clever, lovely girl in the world. But we're so *young*. Suppose we can't cope on our own?"

"Don't be silly," Holly said. "Of course you can cope. Why don't you come round and talk to Mia?"

James shook his head again. "I can't bear to see her cry. I'm going to call her and tell her it's off." He pulled out his phone – but before he could do anything, *Holly's* phone rang.

It was Poppy. "Hey!" she said. "The cakes are all on the stand. They look fabulous. You've got to come and see them!"

"I – " 'I can't come,' Holly was going to say.

But then she had an idea. If James and Mia *saw* each other, they might stop being so silly. If James came into the tent and Mia was there, then maybe …

"Get my family into the tent," she whispered to Poppy. "*All* of them."

Poppy didn't understand. "I thought it was going to be a surprise."

"This is more important," Holly said. "Do it – *please!*"

She put her phone away and turned to James. "Don't call Mia yet," she said. "There's something I want to show you."

Chapter 8

Disaster!

James frowned. "What is it?"

"It's something in the tent," Holly said. "You *must* see it before you talk to Mia. But we have to be quick. Can we go in your car?"

James nodded slowly. "OK. I'll put your bike in the back."

They drove off to Holly's house and parked outside.

"I'm not coming in," said James.

"Just to the garden," Holly said. "We'll go in the side gate. Come on."

The tent was so big it almost filled the back garden. There were lights inside and Holly could hear her mum and dad talking.

"Come on!" she said to James. And she opened the front flap of the tent.

The cupcake tower was all set up in the middle of the tent. It was stunning. Its silver paint glittered brightly. The pink and white cupcakes looked fresh and pretty. The little silver balls on top were gleaming in the light.

"WOW!" said James.

"WOW!" said another voice, at exactly the same time.

It was Mia. She was standing on the other side of the tent, still in her wedding dress. She looked beautiful.

"Oh, *Mia!*" said James.

"Oh, *James!*" said Mia.

They sounded as if their hearts were breaking.

'Oh no!' thought Holly. 'It's not going to work!' If they spoke to each other, the wedding would be off. Holly jumped in between them and started talking – fast!

"Do you know how many cupcakes there are?" she babbled. "A **thousand**! Everyone in my class made some! We had to work it out very carefully – "

"Not carefully enough!" said Bella's voice from the tent flap. She came racing in, shaking her head.

"What's the matter?" asked Holly.

Bella frowned. "When I made the stand, I forgot how heavy the cakes would be. They weigh over 60 kilos! And that means – "

She didn't have time to finish. There was a loud **CREAK!** and the cupcake tower tilted forward. Then – **SNAP! SNAP!! SNAP!!!** The silver layers started breaking off – and cupcakes went everywhere.

They flew through the air, on to the floor and the tables. There were little silver balls all over the carpet and sugar flowers on the chairs. Splodges of icing hit the lights and the sides of the tent.

The biggest one of all landed on the front of Mia's wedding dress.

"Disaster!" shouted Tom.

Poppy screamed. Bella hid her face in her hands. Holly's dad stared helplessly at the mess and her mum gave a loud shriek - and fainted.

Mia and James looked round at the mess. Then they looked at each other.

"We better get to work," James said.

Mia nodded. "Let's get Mum out of the way first."

They carried her into the house. Then Mia put on an apron and fetched a mop and bucket. "I'll start on the cleaning," she said.

James picked up the bits of the cupcake stand. "I think I can weld this together," he said. "I'll go and get my kit." He looked round at Holly and her friends. "See how many cakes you can rescue."

They all worked very hard. Poppy and Holly collected up all the cakes that were still good to eat. Mia and Tom cleaned up the tent. And Bella handed bits of metal to James, so he could weld the stand together.

By midnight, everything looked beautiful. The carpet was spotless. The tables and chairs were clean. Mia had washed and dried all the tablecloths. Poppy put all the good cakes back on the stand and filled the empty spaces with flowers so the cupcake tower was even more stunning than before.

"Let's eat the broken cakes," Mia said.

She and James made a big pot of coffee and fetched some plates. When Holly's mum and dad came back into the tent, everyone was sitting down eating cake and drinking coffee.

"It's all cleared up!" said Mum. "I can't believe it. I didn't know where to start."

"But Mia and James did," said Holly. "They were the only ones who knew how to cope. They're a great team."

James put an arm round Mia. "We can cope with anything," he said. "As long as we're together. Right, Mia?"

"Right!" said Mia. And she gave him a huge smile.

Chapter 9

Happy Ever After – With Cupcakes

So there was a wedding after all.

Mia pinned some pink roses over the stain on her dress and it looked even better than before. Everyone loved the cupcake tower and there were plenty of cakes to go round. People were full of chicken and salad and chocolate pudding and no one wanted *ten* cupcakes.

When James and Mia had gone off on their honeymoon, Holly called her friends and they came round to finish the cakes.

"They're *scrummy!*" said Poppy.

Holly looked up at the stand. "I'm going to have one of these when I get married," she said. "But it's going to be even *bigger*."

"Cool!" said Bella. "Can I make it?"

They all looked at her. "Suppose it collapses?" said Poppy.

Bella grinned. "It won't! James is going to teach me how to weld. So my next stand will be super-strong."

"Fantastic!" said Holly. She closed her eyes and imagined herself in a lace wedding dress, standing beside a giant cupcake tree – with a beautiful sugar butterfly on every cake.

2,000 of them!

Our books are tested
for children and young people by
children and young people.

Thanks to everyone who consulted on
a manuscript for their time and effort in
helping us to make our books better
for our readers.